MW00955380

Make Room for Jasper

Make Room for Jasper

LIFE LESSONS FROM DOGS SERIES

JOANN NEVE, M.Ed.

Illustrated by Janelle Edstrom

PALMETTO
PUBLISHING

Charleston, SC
www.PalmettoPublishing.com

Make Room for Jasper
Copyright © 2021 by Joann Neve

All rights reserved
No portion of this book may be reproduced, stored in a retrieval system, or transmitted
in any form by any means—electronic, mechanical, photocopy, recording, or other—except
for brief quotations in printed reviews, without prior permission of the author.

First Edition

Hardcover ISBN: 978-1-63837-637-8
Paperback ISBN: 978-1-63837-846-4
eBook ISBN: 978-1-63837-847-1

Joann Neve

Visit the author's website at
JOANNNEVE.COM

Joann is a talented dog trainer who has shared her love of dogs with the beautifully written story about belonging, being accepted, and finding a new friend. Joann's writing helps you identify with Fergie's desire for a friend but finds out a friend can become family. This is a must-read for any reader who loves dogs!

—Michelle Bitzer Walgren, M.Ed.

Make Room for Jasper is a fun, nonpreachy way to begin a discussion on blending families! I love that the story flows naturally and doesn't come across as a stilted narrative trying to too hard to get its lesson heard. Instead, it teaches kids in the way they learn, through fun, expressive pictures and a story with meaning and depth beyond the words on the page. My three kids (five, three, and one) loved it and are already asking for more stories about Jasper and Fergie!

—Sara Goudge, MA, Licensed Professional Clinical Counselor (LPCC), child/adolescent therapist, mom of 3

This is a charming children's book written by Joann, a devoted dog mom and trainer. She tells a story of love and trust between a dog and her owner and shows that when they listen to each other, good things happen. Joann shows there is always room in your heart to love one more.

—Debbie Plude, daycare owner

To Mom, who always knew I could;
my daughters, who always challenged me to be better;
and my dogs (all of them) for just being them.

Fergie was a wonderful little puppy.

She had a wonderful new home
and a great new mom.

Coco also lived with Mom. She was old and was sick. She didn't move much and really wasn't much fun at all.

Coco growled at Fergie to keep her away.

Fergie just thought Coco was grumpy.

Fergie had fun with Mom.

Whenever she could, Mom played with Fergie. But she had to work, too, and couldn't be with Fergie all the time.

Days passed, and Fergie tried to keep busy. She played on the deck and with her toys.

She ran up and down the stairs.

And of course, Fergie played with Mom whenever she could.

But Fergie needed more.

She was becoming bored.
She wanted a friend
to play with.

One day, Mom saw Fergie just lying around and not playing much anymore.

Mom knew Fergie was missing her brothers and sisters and needed a friend in the house.

Mom knew just what to do. She made a phone call and then put Fergie in the car for a long ride.

When the car finally stopped,
they were in front of a house that
Fergie had never seen before.

Mom told Fergie they were going into this strange house to meet some new friends.

Fergie was met inside
by six of the biggest
dogs she had ever seen.
She wanted to run back
to the car.

But Fergie trusted Mom and walked with her toward the large pack of dogs.

Mom introduced her to Joey.

Fergie didn't know it, but Mom was going to bring Joey home to be Fergie's new brother.

Or so Mom thought.

Fergie looked around the room. She looked at Joey.

Then she saw *HIM!*

He was the biggest dog in the room. It was *Jasper!*

Fergie's eyes lit up, and her tail started to wag. Fergie darted off to play with this giant of a dog.

Jasper's owners said that he didn't like to play, but Fergie didn't care.

Within minutes Fergie and Jasper were running around the house, jumping, rolling, and playing like they had known each other forever.

The other dogs just stood there and looked on in amazement. Fergie's mom was stunned too.

Seeing this, Mom made a decision. Jasper would be Fergie's new brother! Jasper and Fergie could have fun and play whenever they wanted to.

The three of them happily went home to start their new family.

Adjusting to life with Jasper was interesting and fun.

He was so big; he took up the whole couch. There was almost no room for Fergie.

They couldn't eat together from the same bowl either.

His head was just too big.

Because Jasper's legs were so long,
Fergie could never catch him when
they played in the yard.

But they were inseparable.
They played tug (and sometimes
Fergie would win).

They would explore the yard.
Jasper would always watch to be
sure Fergie was safe.

And of course they both would play with Mom.

They even learned important things together. Mom called it "obedience," but they were just having fun.

They were good pups.

When night came, they would cuddle up with each other to fall asleep.

They were always there for each other.

It never mattered that they were different sizes.

It never mattered that their fur was different. It never mattered that they were different kinds of dogs.

And it never mattered that they had different mom-and-dad dog parents.

They were brother and sister!

And they loved each other for many happy years!

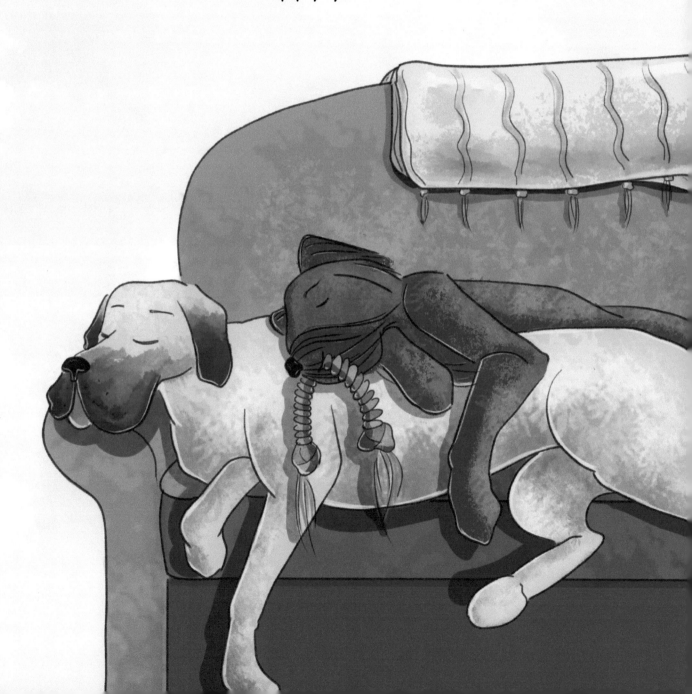

CPSIA information can be obtained
at www.ICGtesting.com
Printed in the USA
BVHW021545050821
613728BV00003B/130